This
Treasure Cove Story
belongs to

M IS FOR MONSTER

A CENTUM BOOK 978-1-912396-08-5
Published in Great Britain by Centum Books Ltd.
This edition published 2018. 1 3 5 7 9 10 8 6 4 2

Centum Books Ltd, 20 Devon Square, Newton Abbot,
Devon, TQ12 2HR, UK.

www.centumbooksltd.co.uk | books@centumbooksltd.co.uk
CENTUM BOOKS Limited Reg.No. 07641486.

A CIP catalogue record for this book is available
from the British Library.

Printed in China.

centum

A Treasure Cove Story

DISNEP·PIXAR

MONSTERS, INC.

M IS FOR MONSTER

By Mike Wazowski
Paintings by Ricky Nierva

A

is for author.
I write *and* I'm cute!

B is for Boo in her monster suit.

 **is for Celia and her lovely hair.**

D is for door.
You scare kids through there.

E is for eyeball. I have only one.

F is for fur and for friendship and fun.

G is for George. Get that sock off his back!

H is for hungry — time
for a sushi snack!

I is for ID card — with my very own name!

J is for jokes. They're
my claim to fame.

 **is for kids. Can you find Boo?**

L is for laughing, a fun thing to do.

 **is for monster. And also for me!**

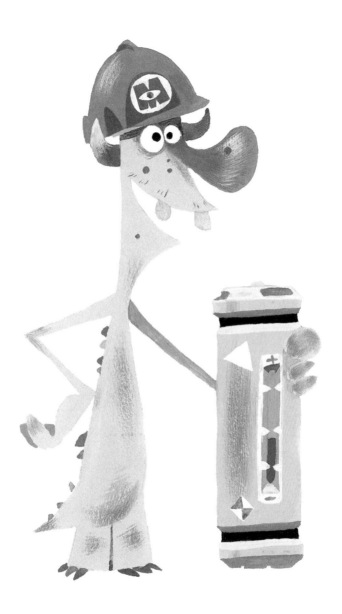

 is for Needleman, as you can see.

O

is for oven gloves. They protect you from stuff.

P is for paperwork.
Roz, that's enough!

Q is for quittin' time, when the workday is through.

R is for Randall. (He'll sneak up on you!)

S is for Sulley,
who's quite overgrown.

T

is for teddy bear.
Boo, get your own!

U is for ugh! That hurt my eye!

V is for very painful. I just might cry.

W is for Waternoose
on the scare floor.

X is for xylophone – and
not too much more.

Y is for Yeti, our chilly new friend.

Z

**is for zzzzzzzzzz,
because this is the end!**

Treasure Cove Stories

1 Three Little Pigs
2 Snow White & The Seven Dwarfs
3 The Fox and the Hound - Hide and Seek
4 Dumbo
5 Cinderella
6 Cinderella's Friends
7 Alice In Wonderland
8 Mad Hatter's Tea Party from Alice In Wonderland
9 Mickey Mouse and his Spaceship
10 Peter Pan
11 Pinocchio
12 Mickey Mouse Flies the Christmas Mail
13 Sleeping Beauty and the Good Fairies
14 The Lucky Puppy
15 Chicken Little
16 Mother Goose
17 Coco
18 Winnie-the-Pooh and Tigger
19 The Sword in the Stone
20 Mary Poppins
21 The Jungle Book
22 Aristocats
23 Lady and the Tramp
24 Bambi
25 Bambi - Friends of the Forest
26 Pete's Dragon
27 Beauty & The Beast - The Teapot's Tale
28 Monsters, Inc. - M is for Monster
29 Finding Nemo
30 The Incredibles
31 The Incredibles - Jack-Jack Attack
32 Ratatouille - Your Friend the Rat
33 Wall-E
34 Up
35 Princess and the Frog

36 Toy Story - The Pet Problem
37 Dora the Explorer - Dora and the Unicorn King
38 Dora the Explorer - Grandma's House
39 Spider-Man - Night of the Vulture!
40 Wreck-it Ralph
41 Brave
42 The Invincible Iron Man - Eye of the Dragon
43 SpongeBob SquarePants - Sponge in Space!
44 SpongeBob SquarePants - Where the Pirates Arrrgh!
45 Toy Story - A Roaring Adventure
46 Cars - Deputy Mater Saves the Day!
47 Spider-Man - Trapped By The Green Goblin
48 Big Hero 6
49 Spider-Man - High Voltage!
50 Frozen
51 Cinderella Is My Babysitter
52 Beauty & The Beast - I Am The Beast
53 Blaze and the Monster Machines - Mighty Monster Machines
54 Blaze and the Monster Machines - Dino Parade!
55 Teenage Mutant Ninja Turtles - Follow The Ninja!
56 I Am A Princess
57 Paw Patrol - The Big Book of Paw Patrol
58 Paw Patrol - Adventures with Grandpa
59 Merida Is My Babysitter
60 Trolls
61 Trolls Holiday Special
62 The Secret Life of Pets
63 Zootropolis
64 Ariel Is My Babysitter
65 Inside Out

66 Belle Is My Babysitter
67 The Lion Guard - Eye In The Sky
68 Moana
69 Finding Dory
70 Guardians of the Galaxy
71 Captain America - High-Stakes Heist!
72 Ant-Man
73 The Mighty Avengers
74 The Mighty Avengers - Lights Out!
75 The Incredible Hulk
76 Shimmer & Shine - Wish upon a Sleepover
77 Shimmer & Shine - Backyard Ballet
78 Paw Patrol - All-Star Pups!
79 Teenage Mutant Ninja Turtles - Really Spaced Out!
80 Cars 2 - Travel Buddies
81 Madagascar
82 Jasmine Is My Babysitter
83 How To Train Your Dragon
84 Shrek
85 Puss In Boots
86 Kung Fu Panda
87 Beauty & The Beast - I Am Belle
88 The Lion Guard - The Imaginary Okapi
89 Thor - Thunder Strike
90 Guardians of the Galaxy -Rocket to the Rescue
91 Nella The Princess Knight - Nella and the Dragon
92 Shimmer & Shine - Treasure Twins!
93 Olaf's Frozen Adventure
94 Black Panther
95 Branch's Bunker Birthday
96 Shimmer & Shine - Pet Talent Show

Book list may be subject to change.

An ongoing series to collect and enjoy!